Sex Comes
to Pemberley

Sex Comes
to Pemberley

Mary Bennet

Winchester, UK
Washington, USA

First published by Bedroom Books, 2014
Bedroom Books is an imprint of John Hunt Publishing Ltd., Laurel House, Station Approach,
Alresford, Hants, SO24 9JH, UK
office1@jhpbooks.net
www.johnhuntpublishing.com
www.bedroom-books.com

For distributor details and how to order please visit the 'Ordering' section on our website.

Text copyright: Mary Bennet 2013

ISBN: 978 1 78279 390 8

A CIP catalogue record for this book is available from the British Library.

Design: Stuart Davies

Printed in the USA by Edwards Brothers Malloy

We operate a distinctive and ethical publishing philosophy in all
areas of our business, from our global network of authors to
production and worldwide distribution.

CONTENTS

For FRL and for
Cassandra, Jane, Elizabeth, Catherine and Lydia
without whom this book could not have been written.

Preface

Pride and Prejudice, the nation's best-loved novel, centres on the Georgian marriage market. How can Mr and Mrs Bennet find rich husbands for their five daughters and in so doing save Mrs Bennet and her daughters from the penury which will result when Mr Bennet dies? Mr Bennet is reasonably wealthy but Longbourn, his family estate, and most of his income will be lost to his family when he moves on.

Why? Because Mr and Mrs Bennet have not managed to have a son and heir. Property in Georgian England was sometimes handed down from male to male and the Bennets' failure to have a son means that Longbourn is 'entailed' and will pass on to a male cousin, Mr Collins.

In the marriage market of Georgian England, both men and women were valued by their estates and their income. Ideally, wealthy men would marry wealthy women. But there was always an X factor: charm and good looks–or what we might now call sex appeal. A really pretty face, if well marketed, was worth a lot of money. And a penniless but charming bounder might use his sexual allure to entrap a rich heiress.

In *Pride and Prejudice* Jane Austen tells how three of the Bennet daughters find husbands. Pretty Jane and witty Elizabeth marry wealthy men, Bingley and Darcy, who both have substantial estates. Loose and lusty Lydia abandons herself to her teenage hormonal drives, runs off with Wickham, a charming philanderer, and is on the brink of becoming a fallen woman when she is saved by the intervention of Darcy, who is about to become her rich brother-in-law. This leaves pretty but delicate Kitty and accomplished but ugly Mary unmarried at the end of the novel.

Sex Comes to Pemberley, while remaining true to the story of

Pride and Prejudice, takes the reader into a world where SEX and the re-imagined sex lives of the five daughters (and their mother) are central not peripheral.

1

Kitty in Love

The autumn afternoon was just beginning to fold the world in its mysterious embrace. Far away in the west the sun was setting and the last glow of the all too fleeting day lingered lovingly on Longbourn and its environs.

The two girls were walking together, hand in hand, enjoying the evening scene and the air which was fresh but not too chilly. Many a time and oft were they wont to walk along the path in order to pay a visit to their aunt, to meet new friends and to have a cosy chat together about matters feminine. It was a merry way, the way to Meryton, which now housed the militia.

Kitty, the eldest of the duo, had recently turned sixteen. Sweet sixteen and never been kissed. Her elder sisters, prim and proper Jane and the ever saucy and sarcastic Elizabeth, always seemed to take the limelight. And even Lydia, dearest Lydia, though the youngest of the family was the taller of the pair and looked the older. 'You must wait your turns,' their mother said. 'We can't have you marrying before your elder sisters.'

Waiting for Jane, who was nearly engaged to that nice Mr Bingley, with, it was rumoured at least £10,000 a year, but perhaps even a little more, was not a problem. Nor would be waiting for Elizabeth, though too high and mighty to accept an honourable proposal from their cousin Mr Collins, be likely to prove a hindrance insurmountable. For Elizabeth, and who could blame her, the grass would always be much greener on the opposite side. And, perhaps, it would be better to marry a soldier with a mere five thousand than a clergyman with twenty, especially a clergyman who was rather plain and read sermons and disapproved of novels.

But who could be expected to wait for Mary? Mary, Mary, quite contrary, and always in the library. No wonder that even Mr Collins had looked afresh at further fields and had chosen Charlotte Lucas. Poor Mary, always at the piano and saying clever things, might have been different had she had the Bennet looks. And always only too ready to bend over backwards just to please her father.

So unlike Lydia. What charm that girl had, despite her lack of years. A truer-hearted lass never drew the breath of life, always with a laugh in her eyes and a frolicsome word on her cherry red lips, a girl lovable in the extreme. Anyway, all the red coats seemed to like her. And to tell the truth, she, Kitty, though the older and the prettier, would never have dared to venture out alone without her little sister.

Girls will be girls and the two sisters were no exception to this golden rule. And the evening walk to Meryton was just such a temptation. At first all the soldiers had looked the same, so bright, so manly and so smartly dressed, and always smiling. But now she and Lydia were starting to make distinctions. Some were little more than boys. There were Watt and Ellis and Thompson and Gibbs. Hardly old enough to have left their village homes. And then there were the officers, Captain Denny and Captain Parker and Colonel Forster and Lydia's favourite, Captain Carter. All manly men and worthy of any girl's attention. And it was said that Colonel Forster might be worth at least twenty or even thirty thousand pounds.

But who was Kitty - for that was the name her friends and family called her? Catherine Bennet, now lost in thought, was in very truth as fair a specimen of English girlhood as anyone could wish to see. She was pronounced beautiful by all who knew her though, as folks often said, she was more a Gardiner than a Bennet. The hint of pallor in her face was almost spiritual in its purity, just given a touch of colour by the tasteful application of Almona Bloom, or Liquid Vegetable Rouge, an invaluable discovery for the improvement of the female person, lent to her by her friend Maria Lucas. But Kitty's rosebud mouth was a genuine Cupid's bow, Greekly perfect. No need for extra colouring there. And when she smiled, her teeth, now regularly cleaned and whitened with that new charcoal powder, were a sight both for sore eyes and to be beholden.

No. Honour where honour is due. There was an innate refinement about Kitty. Had kind fate but willed her to be born a gentlewoman of high degree, perhaps even a Darcy, and had she had her own governess or received the benefit of a good education, Kitty might easily have held her own beside any lord and lady in the land. But it had been God's will to test her and, settling for second best, Kitty was a daughter worth her weight in gold, a ministering angel too, who, when her mother had those nervous fainting fits, was always the first to offer her a cordial and to try hardest to console her.

Mayhap it was this, the life of selflessness, that lent to Kitty's softly featured face at whiles a look, tense with suppressed meaning, that imparted a strange yearning tendency to the beautiful eyes, a charm few could resist, or so her mirror told her. Why have women such eyes of witchery? Kitty's were of the bluest blue, set off by lustrous lashes and dark expressive brows. Time was when those brows were not so dark or so silkily seductive. It was Madame Vera Verity, directress of the Woman Beautiful page of the Lady's Monthly Museum, that Polite Repository of Amusements and Instructions, who had first advised her to try Eyebrowleine which gave her that haunting expression, so becoming in leaders of fashion, and she had never regretted it. There were other helpful hints in the Polite Repository. There was blushing scientifically cured and how to increase your height. And there was you may have a beautiful face but your nose? That would suit Maria Lucas because hers was a button one.

But Kitty's crowning glory was her wonderful wealth of hair. It was dark brown with a natural wave in it. She had trimmed it herself that very morning on account of the new moon and it nestled about her pretty head in a profusion of luxuriant clusters lingering beneath her hat and she had pared her nails too.

'Good evening Sebastian,' Lydia's words, so brash and unbecoming, broke the silence and stopped her reverie and a tell-tale flush crept into Kitty's delicate cheeks so that she looked so lovely in her sweet girlish shyness that of a surety God's fair land of England did not hold her equal. Yes, it was one of her favourites, Captain Wallace. But how could Lydia so openly call him by his first name? What a flirt that girl was. Even young married women were not so brash. For her, he would always be Captain Wallace, and she knew from his eyes and from his smile that she and not lumpy Lydia was the one that he really yearned for and adored.

'Good evening Miss Lydia and Miss Kitty,' the captain jocularly replied. Kitty's dignity told her to be silent and to check the words about to come to her tongue. Silence at times like this was golden. She knew right well, no one better, what made Lydia speak so crudely. For just a moment, she, Catherine Bennet, imagined herself yielding to him, he taking her in his sheltering arms, straining her to him in all the strength of his refined but deeply passionate nature and comforting her with a long, long kiss. For such a one she yearned that autumn evening. But it was not to be. Captain Wallace did not stop, but walked on briskly.

The visit to the Phillips proved to be a breath of the freshest air. Much had been done and much more said in the regiment since their last visit the preceding Wednesday. Uncle Phillips was troubled by the ague, from too much wine the doctor said. Several of the officers had dined lately and a private had been flogged and it had been hinted that Colonel Forster was soon to be married. And there was talk of an exciting newcomer. A Mr, or was it even a Captain, Wickham.

Well, if wishes were horses only beggars could ride, but this time their dearest wish was to be answered. Back on the way to Longbourn, outside the Meryton town hall, who should they encounter? None other than their old friend Captain Denny. And walking with him was a fellow officer who took their breath away. Both girls were struck with the stranger's air. A manly man, most gentlemanlike. And in his full regalia. Captain Denny addressed the girls directly. 'May I introduce my old friend, Wickham, Captain Wickham.'

And straightway Kitty realised that she had been wise to wait. Here was her beau ideal, a man ready to lay down his rare and wondrous love straight at her feet. And even while she gazed, her heart went pit-a-pat. Yes, it was she, Catherine Bennet, he was looking at, and there was meaning in that look. 'You are lovely Kitty Bennet, and I live to love and serve you,' he told her with his eyes. Eyes which burned right through her as though they would search her through and through and read her very soul. Wonderful eyes they were, superbly expressive. But could you really trust them? No matter. It was he who mattered and there was joy on her face because she wanted him and because she felt instinctively that he was like no other. The very heart of the girl-woman went out to him, her dream husband, because she knew on the instant that it was he. If he had suffered, more sinned against than sinning, or even, even, if he had been himself a sinner, wicked Wickham, a wicked man, she cared not. Besides, if there were wounds that wanted healing with heartbalm, she was a womanly woman not like other flighty girls, unhygienic and unfeminine, that he might previously have known. She would forgive all, give all, and make him forget those moments from the past. Then he could crush her soft body to him and he would love her for herself and for herself alone.

Kitty took off her hat for a moment to settle her hair and a prettier, daintier head of nut-brown tresses was never seen on a girl's shoulders – a radiant little vision, in sooth, almost maddening in its sweetness. You would have to travel many a long mile beyond Meryton before you found a head of hair the like of that. She could almost see the swift answering flash of admiration in his eyes that set her tingling in every nerve. He was eying her as a fox might eye a rabbit. Her woman's instinct told her that she had raised the very devil in him and at the thought a burning scarlet swept from throat to brow till the lovely colour of her face became a glorious rose. If ever there was undisguised passion in a man's gaze, it was there plain to be seen. It is for you, Kitty Bennet and you know it. She smiled, a smile reinforced by the whitest of white teeth.

Captain Denny, chatting to Lydia, nodded and Kitty sensed that they were about to part, hearts perhaps never to meet again, broken cruelly and suddenly asunder.

And then a rocket sprang and bang shot blind blank. It was the fireworks, close by, the fireworks at Meryton. She had forgotten that this was Guy Fawkes Night. Together they all gazed up in rapture. And. Oh. Oh. OH! Then a Roman candle burst and it was like a sigh of Oh! And they all cried Oh! OH! in raptures, and out of it gushed a stream of rain gold hair threads and they shed, and Ah! They were all greeny dewy stars falling with golden, Oh so lovely, OH. OH, so soft, so sweet, so, so ...

And then, and then, a sign on high as if from the almighty. There, close beside them, there burst into flame and fire, in the form of a five pointed cross, Kitty's star, her own star, yes, a five piece Catherine wheel, and she gazed on it and then she gazed into his eyes, his beautiful eyes caught in fire light and they told her yes, yes, yes. And in return she imagined herself holding out her slender arms to him and feeling his lips laid on her brow as she gave out a little cry, Oh! Oh! OH! Her cry, the cry of a young girl's love, innocent and pure, a strangled cry wrung from her and echoing down the ages. And then the kiss. The first long, long kiss, that would mark for them their eternal betrothal.

Then Kitty coughed, a small cough, delicate but deadly. She knew and he knew that it was the cough of a young consumptive. She raised her eyes and turned them to him and only then he realised that in that face, so pure, so spiritual, there was both love and death. White hot passion was in his face, passion as silent and as eternal as the grave.

Such was the scene there in the gathering Meryton twilight.

2

Lusty Lydia

My dear Kitty,

I think you should be the first to know. I am sending this by Wickham's man, Hobson, who has promised to deliver it secretly to Jennings. Hold it to your bosom and your heart. You and you alone will always be the sole possessor of my history.

After we left Meryton, things happened so very quickly. But I always knew that I was Wickham's favourite. I could tell it from the way he looked at me that first moment when Captain Denny introduced him to us at the Meryton fireworks display. But it did come as a slight surprise when, quite suddenly, he suggested that we should leave Brighton and the militia and head for Gretna Green. How, how very romantic. Our secret dream come true.

But to tell the truth, I was already bored with Brighton, the camp nothing but a ruin, and when he proposed to me I barely had time to put together a few things, including that new lace gown – the one with the embroidered bodice – and we were off in the post chaise which he had hired.

It was early morning when we left and as the sky darkened late that afternoon, Wickham told me that he knew a small inn on the outskirts of London where we might spend the night. By now I was starting to feel nervous, very nervous, but he assured me that the landlady, a Mrs Brown, whom he knew well, would make me feel at home. It was a lovely warm welcome, with a fire burning in the grate and a bowl of negus waiting there in readiness. I was a little surprised to find that his Mrs Brown had clearly been expecting us. And after we had dined, she suggested that her maid, a pretty young woman called Phoebe, should take me to my room. Phoebe took me up a flight of stairs to a small but neat room in which there was a handsome large bed.

To slip over matters of no importance to the main of my story, I started to feel tearful at the idea of spending a whole night completely alone in a strange inn, and Miss Phoebe, observing both my tears and my reluctance to prepare for bed, came up to me and hugged me and beginning with unpinning my handkerchief and gown, soon encouraged me to go on with undressing myself; and, blushing at now seeing myself naked to my shift, and shivering with the cold, I hurried to get under the bedclothes and out of sight.

But Phoebe laughed and it was not long before she placed herself by my side and much to my surprise, still giggling, began embracing me and kissing. This was new, this was odd, but interpreting it as nothing but pure kindness, I was determined not to be behindhand with her, and returned her kisses with perfect innocence.

Encouraged by this, her hands became extremely free, and wandered over my whole body, with touches, squeezes, pressures, that did not disturb but rather warmed and surprised me with their novelty. A little anxious, but not entirely displeased, I lay there all tame and passive, whilst her freedoms raised no other emotion but those of a strange, new pleasure. Every part of me was open and exposed to the licentious courses of her hands, which, like a warming fire, ran over my whole body, and thawed all coldness as they went.

My breasts, which as you know, have only just begun to show themselves, amused her hands awhile, till, slipping down lower, over a smooth track, she could just feel the soft silky down that had but a few months before put forth and garnished the mount pleasant of those parts we seldom touch and never speak of. And then. What an exquisite sensation and in the seat of what had always been a place of almost total innocence and privacy. 'Oh! what a charming creature you are! What a happy man will he be that first makes a woman of you! Oh! that I were a man for your sake! Lucky Captain Wickham,' Phoebe said. And then, rather suddenly, she left me.

For a long while I lay wide awake. In the distance I could just hear voices and other sounds of revelry. Then I could hear footsteps on the stair. Then all went still and quiet. 'Where will Wickham sleep?' I wondered. He had promised that after a day or two in London we would head for Gretna Green where we would be safely married. But now I was even more wide awake and gave scarcely a thought to Gretna. Perhaps I even moaned or sighed a little, just a little.

Well, anyway, there was a tap on the door and before I had the time to rise, it opened and there was George, a candle in his hand, my George, my very own Adonis. And in the candlelight, with a smile full of meaning, he took me gently by the hand, and said, 'Don't cry my dear, for a while I will rest here beside you.' Then, without waiting for my answer, he doused the candle and slipped in beside me. And Kitty, dear Kitty, he was already almost naked. In a moment his lips were glued to mine and we lay together trembling.

My bosom was now quite bare, and rising in the warmest throbs, presented to his feeling hands the firm hard swell of my young breasts. But even their pleasing resistance to the touch could not bribe his restless hands, quicker, rougher, and even more assured and impatient than had been Phoebe's, from roving. At first my fears made me mechanically tighten my thighs and hold my legs together, but the very touch of his hand insinuated between them, opened a way for what I now must call the main attack, though at first it was a most welcome and tender invasion. Gretna Green was far away and we were now both too highly wound up to bear any kind of a delay and in a moment, my Captain Wickham, ever the soldier, had guided with his hand the engine of his love as at a breach made ready to receive him. Or, Kitty, so I thought.

But when I felt that stiff hard thing battering against my tenderest part, imagine to yourself his and my surprise, when we found, that even after several vigorous pushes, which hurt me extremely, it had made not the least impression.

I moaned and tenderly complained that I could bear the battering no longer and I begged him to desist. He did so reluctantly and we lay still together for what seemed an age. I wondered if, despite my height, I might be still too young – but soon a pleasing drowsy warmth replaced the pain and once again I hugged him closely to me.

He tried again, still no admittance, still no penetration. And, Kitty, though my love had helped me to bear the pain almost without a groan, he hurt me more and more. At length, after repeated fruitless trials, he lay down beside me panting. I sighed a little. Then he kissed away my falling tears, and asked me tenderly what was the meaning of so much complaining? I wondered if it might be the vastness of what I think of now as his great love machine. Might I have to wait until I met another, slighter lover? We lay together for what seemed another age. Then George, for now I always call him George, began to smother me with kisses and sighs and I knew that I must submit myself entirely to the power of love.

He told me to have patience and that, as he loved me dearly, he would be as mindful of not hurting me as he would be of not injuring himself. Then he resumed battle but with less, much less, spontaneity. First he stood up and away and placed one of the pillows from the great bed under my thighs, to give himself a somewhat more favourable elevation. Then, spreading wide my legs, and placing himself standing between them, he made another rough assault. At first my point of entry seemed so small, that I could scarce believe that we could ever be well matched. He paused, then looked, then felt and seemed to satisfy himself before driving on again with fury. This put me to such intolerable pain, from the separation of the sides of that soft passage by such a hard thick body, that I could have screamed out. But, as I was unwilling to alarm the house, I held in my breath, and crammed the sheet, which was turned up over my face, into my mouth, and bit it through in the agony. At length, the tender texture of the tract gave way to his fierce tearing and rending as he thrust himself further and further into me until, no longer his own master, his great member began exerting itself with a kind of native rage, and having its own will, broke in, George carrying all before him, and with one violent merciless lunge, he thrust it up to the very hilt in me. Then all my resolution deserted me: I screamed out, and fainted away with the sharpness of the pain. When I recovered my senses, I found myself in the arms of the sweet relenting murderer of my virginity. My eyes, moistened with tears, and languishingly turned upon him, seemed to reproach him with his cruelty, and to ask him, if such were always the rewards of love.

But my sweet George, to whom I was now infinitely endeared by his complete triumph over my lost maidenhead, kissed away my tears, and employed himself with so much sweetness, so much warmth, to soothe, to caress, and comfort me in my soft complainings, which breathed, indeed, more love than resentment, that I presently drowned all sense of pain in the pleasure of feeling him and of knowing that though there would be no Gretna, he would be always mine, and that he would be the absolute disposer of my happiness, and, in one phrase, my fate.

I was still too sore and tender to encourage George to make yet another trial. And he, in his good nature, relented. We lay together in each other's arms throughout the remainder of the night. The next morning I found that I could hardly stir or even walk across the room, so George ordered first breakfast and then luncheon to be brought to me at my bedside. At first I could not eat, but that afternoon my appetite returned and after getting down the wing of a fowl, and three or four glasses of red wine, brought to me by my adored one, I felt that I had left behind my girlhood and was now a new woman. The pain, if only momentarily, was gone.

After all but the wine was taken away by the now ever-smiling Phoebe, George, almost impudently asked leave to come to bed with me once again and reading the welcome in my eyes, accordingly fell to undressing. With eyes downcast, I watched and could not see the progress without strange emotions of both fear and pleasure, devouring all his naked charms with only two eyes, when I could have wished them at least an hundred for the fuller enjoyment of the gaze.

Oh Kitty. If I could only paint his figure for you as I saw it then. Before me a whole length of an all-perfect manly beauty in full view. Think of his face, a face which you know well, without a fault, glowing with all the opening bloom and verdant freshness of manly youth on the very cusp of its maturity. Then a neck exquisitely turned, connecting his head to a body of the most perfect form, in which all the strength of manhood was concealed. And the symmetry of his limbs, his thighs, finely fashioned, and with a florid glossy roundness, gradually tapering away to the knees. I could not, without some remains of terror, some tender emotions too, fix my eyes on that terrible machine, which had, not long before, with such fury broke into, torn, and almost ruined those soft, tender parts of mine, that had not yet done smarting with the effects of its rage. But now I beheld it, seemingly crest fallen, reclining with its half-caped vermilion head over one of his thighs, quiet, pliant, and to all appearances incapable of the mischiefs and cruelty it had previously committed.

He was soon back in bed with me now in broad daylight as

he laid his naked glowing body next to mine. And, oh Kitty, what pain could stand before a pleasure so transporting? I felt no more the smart of my wounds below; but, curling round him I returned his strenuous embraces and kisses with fervour and a gusto only known to true love, and to which mere lust could never rise. Mid pain and pleasure, I now stifled my cries, and bore him with the passive fortitude of a heroine. Soon his thrusts became ever more and more furious, and his cheeks were flushed with an even deeper scarlet than his uniform. And after some dying sighs, and an agonizing shudder, he experienced that ecstatic final pleasure, which I was yet in too much pain to share.

Then we spent the whole afternoon, till dinner time in a continued circle of love delights, kissing, turtle-billing, toying, and all the rest of the feast. At length, supper was served. George ate with a very good appetite, and seemed charmed to see me eat.

But this morning when I woke, I found my beloved no longer there beside me. As daylight hardened on the wall, I began to fear that the vicious rumours I had heard in Meryton and Brighton might be true. Was my Wickham no more than a virgin violator and was I now a fallen woman? I had time on my own to ponder what had been and what might yet be to come. And Kitty, dear Kitty, I realised that the hours of pain and sweet delight that I have just had with my George in London, whatever the outcome, have shown me the insipidity of the life I left behind me far, far away in Longbourn. And even if I am now ruined, the ruin will have been well worth the price of such an ennobling, even if transient pleasure. Was it father who said that a single crowded hour of life is worth an age without a name?

I am, though now fully a woman, your ever loving sister, Lydia

3

Mary, Mary, Quite Contrary

I wish that either my father or my mother, or indeed both of them, as they were in duty both equally bound to it, had minded what they were about when they set out to beget me. For from the very moment that my father's animal spirits entered the alien territory of my mother's – dare I say it – aposiopesis, – the fortunes of the whole house of Bennet were to be in turmoil. My father, sometimes a wit but never a mathematician, had estimated the odds at eight to one that this time the infant homunculus would be a boy. And from the moment of my conception I had set out to oblige. Had I not been placed under such unnatural pressure, I am verily persuaded that I should have made quite a different figure in the world from that which the reader is now about to discover.

For a full ten months, yes ten, the family and indeed the whole neighbourhood had waited on tenterhooks, hoping that the infant in my mother's womb would be the saviour of the family, the long-awaited son and heir who would bring about the ending of the entail. Early on my mother had intimated that this pregnancy felt quite different.

When I, Mary Tristana Bennet, did eventually arrive in this scurvy and disastrous world, there I was, an *almost* perfect specimen and a miracle of nature, consisting of skin, hair, fat, flesh, veins, arteries, ligaments, nerves, cartilages, bones, marrow, brains, glands, humours, and other articulations— and in all senses of the word, as much and as truly a fellow-creature to be welcomed into this world as any peer of England. But the entire welcoming party were concerned with but one small detail missing from the afore-mentioned list.

Yes. Genitalia. And it took but a cursory glance to realise that I was, despite all my efforts to combat the workings of Mother Nature, yet another girl.

When, later, the gaze eventually turned upwards to my face, the realisation came that this girl was not to be another Bennet beauty. 'An imbalance, I fear, between the yin and the yang,' said our family physician, Dr Slop, who had recently arrived back from China. So there I was, an image more frightful than the imagination could paint, or pen describe, but I will try.

Even in the cradle my head was somewhat too large, my eyes misaligned and a little too small and, though only just in evidence, my tresses were a very coarse black. My slightly humped back, one shoulder lower than the other, was not observed until when, some ten months later, I began to crawl. And it is rumoured, though I suspect that this may be a retrospective fabrication, that I was born with a full set of teeth. In brief, I must have been a horrid sight to the wary, let alone the unwary visitor.

Now here, dear reader, here is a space for you to draw me as I have described myself and as you have imagined me.

Now picture that on a crisp new £10 note.

My mother looked at me, grimaced, and passed me to the wet nurse and that was to be the end of our bonding. My father lowered his eyes and retired to his library. For a full ten months I had striven to become a son and heir and now ahead lay a lifetime of trying to be a pretty daughter.

Though I now hate Art, as a toddler I surrounded myself with Patches, Powder, Pomatum and Paint.

When I was six, I heard my aunt Phillips whispering to my mother some words about 'a governess' and a few weeks later, my father procured the services of an able-handed preceptoress to superintend my education. What is a preceptoress? You may well ask. 'Preceptoress' was the family word for a peripatetic governess, that is a governess who shared her favours and her skills but did not live at home but in the village. My father, weighed down by the entail, said we could not afford a live-in governess and had to make do with second best.

But Miss Dickins was an excellent tutor and I a willing pupil. Under her instruction, I quickly learned to read and write and soon started work on singing, drawing, dancing, playing the harp, the flute, the violin, the pianoforte and the dulcimer and learning several languages, so it was not long before I had gained the reputation of being quite the most accomplished young lady in the village. Only later did I realise that my aunt had meant that I was likely to become what she liked to term 'a maid not vendible', and that I was destined to **become** a governess and that my father had hired Miss Dickins in the hope that she would hand on to me the essentials of her trade.

Miss Dickins, who confided in me that she loved the local curate, supplemented her more conventional tutoring by directing me through a programme of moral readings, which she liked to call the 'Paths of Virtue', readings carefully selected for the improving of both of our minds. Day by day, my nature, naturally morose, was becoming increasingly more amiable and hers, though naturally compliant, was becoming ever and ever more steadfast. We seemed to be very near perfection when, quite suddenly, Life triumphed over Art and Education and my seemingly worthy preceptoress deserted me. It happened shortly before I had attained my thirteenth year. I will always remember her last words. 'My dear Mary' she said, `Good night t'ye.' And that very evening she eloped with Grandison, our gardener.

Soon after the elopement, I discovered comfort-eating and was seldom without my tin of cakes and biscuits.

Alone without my governess, I worked hard at my drawing, but, with little talent and no tutor, soon realised that I was a failure. Hours and hours spent at the pianoforte were more productive, and, as the years rolled by, from time to time, I would be allowed to entertain, although from the perpetual buzzing chatter and the yawning and the muted but relieved applause, I knew that no one ever really cared or even listened. My mother, who had little time for cleverness or musicality, preferred and indeed much encouraged the flightiness of my two younger sisters.

So I set out to woo and win my father. I joined him in his library, generally hunched unnoticed under the great table, and selected Fordyce's 'Sermons for Young Women', a text introduced to me by my dear Miss Dickins as the work most likely to impress, copying out and learning long passages by heart. Then I tried to find ways to introduce into our daily conversation some of the more aphoristic clichés – about pride and vanity and the vicissitudes of fate and fortune. My sisters decided that I must be 'very clever', but from my father's constant mockery, I knew that he was not impressed.

Then I discovered Shakespeare. My father had just purchased Malone's handsome ten-volume edition of the plays. I started on the comedies, reading them avidly, still crouched under the great table in the library. Here was no easy moralizing. Here was no path to virtue. Here was a mirror of the goings-on at Longbourn.

I first read *The Tempest* and immediately was in a familiar world. There was I with my father, Prospero, happily in exile in his library with his books. And Miranda? Alas. I was not Miranda. Any of the other four might well have been Miranda, as Ferdinand shifted seamlessly from being Bingley, to Colonel Forster to Wickham or any of the men from the militia, before he metamorphosed suddenly and quite unexpectedly into Fitzwilliam Darcy. And me? Yes, of course, I was destined to be Caliban, the thing of darkness longing, longing to be acknowledged his.

Most of Shakespeare's comedies tell stories of how fathers, alive or dead, struggle to marry off their daughters. Some of the daughters are submissives, like sisters Jane and Kitty; others are dominants like Elizabeth and Lydia. But who was I? What roles were there for ugly Mary? Don John seemed a kindred spirit. So I determined to abandon virtue and to play at being villainous.

It was at about this time that I first tried my hand at pogonotomy, practising with a cut throat razor (a genuine Huntsman, made in Sheffield) which I had borrowed from my father. I kept it in my cake tin, under the library table with my books.

When the militia arrived in Meryton, puberty seemed to hit Longbourn like a rash. My younger sisters instantaneously came on heat and started to strut about like little bitches. All was wars and lechery. Lydia and Kitty now spent their days walking endlessly into Meryton, flirting outrageously with the military, and table-talk soon became 'Captain Carter this' and 'Colonel Forster that.' Sometimes I joined them on their walks and I watched while lust, with his potato finger, tickled them and drove them on and on in their pursuit of folly. They rapidly became the subject of much gossip, reviled as 'hussies, tarts and wicked little minxes'. But my father, still pretending to remain aloof, dismissed them fondly as 'the silliest girls in town'. My mother, who confessed to having been rather fond of red coats in her youth, and realising that beggars can't be choosers, snooped about the village and came home with tales to tell of incomes and estates hidden behind the bright and gaudy military regalia. 'It would appear to be a truth, that when the army comes to Meryton, they quickly lose all sense of king and country and turn their attention to finding pretty wives,' said my father.

By now my own puberty had arrived, its outward sign a particularly virulent strain of acne.

The militia were briefly forgotten when the Bingleys moved into Netherfield. I watched and waited as, egged on by my mother, my sister Jane (outwardly a cross between a box of chocolates and a spaniel, but in reality something of a little serpent) was sent forth to trap our new neighbour, Mr Bingley. Poor Bingley, a man without a brain cell in his head or a real bone in his body, would have been easy prey but for the interventions from his envious, spiteful and malicious sisters and from his friend, the mighty Mr Darcy.

Right from the start, Fitzwilliam Darcy, he of the sneer and haughty grimace, looked down on the Bennet family, his nose suggesting that he had just discovered something very, very nasty. Darcy was a proud man, used to high society and the polite attentions of genuinely accomplished women. So I saw and took my chance to play at anti-cupid and to throw my small spanner in the marriage works. Whenever possible, I took on the role of 'clever Mary', clever, fat and spotted Mary, feeding assemblies at Netherfield and at Longbourn with a battery of Fordyce's more boring platitudes. And, when I saw an opportunity, I stepped in between Jane and Elizabeth and the family's hopes by dominating the evening soirees at the piano. I even sang from time to time and, alarmingly, my voice began to break.

I had realised that, despite her outward show, our little Lizzie had been stricken by Fitzwilliam Darcy the moment when, at a ball in Meryton, he had found her to be just 'barely tolerable'. And, she, a bright-eyed little bottled spider, determined on revenge and immediately set out to weave a web in which to catch him.

'Can you imagine that face looking at you day after day over the breakfast table?' her friend Charlotte Lucas had asked her, kindly trying to assuage the hurt caused by Darcy's sneering snub. The answer, of course, was that any of the girls in Meryton would have endured any kind of face if the face owned Pemberley and was worth even a fraction of his ten thousand pounds a year.

But, ironically, it was horse-faced Charlotte who reneged on all her own comforting advice and in doing so stepped in between me and *my* hopes. I will be brief.

Soon after Darcy's put down of Elizabeth, a letter for my father arrived from a cousin, a Mr William Collins. It announced with some pomposity an intended visit to Longbourn, which he now regarded as his ancestral home. For Mr Collins, recently orphaned and ordained, was to be the beneficiary of the dreaded entail. No doubt he had heard tales of the bright and brilliant Bennet beauties, and the letter made it clear that he was offering my father, not just an olive branch, but the chance to rid himself of one of his five daughters.

Negotiations, presided over by my mother, soon began. 'Just right for our Elizabeth,' I heard her whisper to my father. But when, eventually, our cousin arrived and announced himself, the verdict was unanimous. He was rather plain. 'So plain that I cannot even bear too look at him,' said Lydia.

On discovering that Jane was more or less affianced to

beef-witted Bingley, our Mr Collins made, as my mother had predicted, a play for little Lizzie who had by then set her sights much higher and turned him down imperiously. When the marriage negotiation party met that afternoon, my mother took the floor:

'I am not going to force you, child, but want to know now what your resolution is, having received such a handsome and honourable proposal. If *you* don't accept him, Kitty or Lydia may. Will you accept the Reverend Collins to be your lawful, wedded husband?' asks my mother.

'My awful wedded husband! Over my dead body,' Elizabeth instantly replies. At which my mother's nerves begin to plague her. 'I want you to know Elizabeth, that if you turn down Mr Collins, I, for one, will never, ever speak to you again.' To emphasise her distress, she then faints, and is so intent to show her disapproval that she succumbs to not just one, but to a succession of her fainting fits, so that she has scarcely patience enough to recover from one before she falls into yet another.

'An unhappy alternative is now before you, Elizabeth,' says my father, in between the fainting and the fits, 'from this day you must be a stranger to one of your parents. Your mother will never see you again if you do *not* marry Mr. Collins, and I will never see you again if you *do*.'

When my mother eventually recovered consciousness and heard that not only Lizzie but also Kitty and Lydia had turned down Mr C, she whispered to my father: 'Mr Bennet, it might yet be a blessing in disguise, he could be just what we are looking for, for Mary,' And, in truth, both his letter and his conversation had seemed to echo the words and sentiments of my alter-ego, the Reverend James Fordyce. But in no time, my father's verdict on the proposal to Elizabeth had spread throughout the village. It soon became another of his famous witticisms. And I guess that did for me, for shortly afterwards, the engagement between our cousin and Charlotte Lucas was announced. Imagine a lifetime of seeing that face across the breakfast table, listening to its pomposities and helping it to write its sermons. I came to see it as a most fortunate deliverance.

And, besides, by now I had discovered self-pleasuring, and with Shakespeare and my cakes and biscuits and my razor saw no need for an immediate entry into marriage.

But I was telling you about the progress of the family's attempt to trap bone-headed Bingley. All had seemed to be going well when, at my mother's insistence, Jane rode by horse to Netherfield Park, caught a very convenient cold and was forced to stay there for several days and nights. Soon Elizabeth, in hot pursuit of Mr Darcy, had joined her there and the setting seemed ripe for romance.

So when the pair returned to Longbourn, we all awaited a visit from the boneless one and a request for at least one daughter's hand in marriage. But my mother and my father (and, indeed, sister Elizabeth), had not reckoned on the nature of the opposition. In Jane's absence Bingley had easily been persuaded by his friend Darcy that he had misread the signs. Jane was not in love with him. No. She was a charming country girl whose charm, though it indicated a generous nature, meant nothing and, moreover, given the entail and her father's poverty and her mother's crude vulgarity (which even the bone-headed one had noticed) it was time to do away with country pleasures and to return to London. Which they did. And almost immediately, news came that the militia were to be transferred to Brighton. The future for the Bennet family was looking rather bleak.

So back again to Shakespeare, whose heroine in 'All's Well' is prepared to cross great continents in pursuit of her beloved. And in no time not one but three of the Bennet daughters had set out in their attempts to hunt down their prey, to secure their destinies and to bring to an end the curse of the entail.

The first to go was Jane. She was despatched to London to stay with our aunt and uncle Gardiner but she, alas, lacking the enterprise of Shakespeare's Helena, just waited. She waited and waited, hoping, perhaps, for a visit from the boneless bone-head. She even called upon his sisters, perhaps in the hope that they might energise their brother. Maliciously they told her that he was soon to be engaged to Mr Darcy's sister. So she returned to Longbourn where she tended to sit all day like Patience on her famous monument.

Meanwhile Elizabeth set off to stay with Mr and Mrs Collins at the parsonage in Hunsford. All at Longbourn were bemused. What possible pleasure could any spirited young woman take in six weeks of the company of Mr. Collins? And delicacy, apart from any other consideration, should have kept her well away from Hunsford. But Elizabeth had somehow discovered that Lady Catherine de Bourgh was Mr. Collins's neighbour, and that her nephew, Mr. Darcy, would almost certainly be at nearby Rosings while Elizabeth was visiting the parsonage. And some weeks later a letter from Charlotte to her mother arrived to say that Elizabeth had indeed been visited by Mr Darcy several times and on one occasion they had walked out together. My mother excitedly awaited an announcement, but soon after Lizzie returned home, empty-handed, sullen and uncommunicative.

But Elizabeth did not join Jane patiently on the monument. No. Almost immediately she accepted an invitation from our aunt and uncle, the Gardiners, to make a visit to the Lake District. Lizzie had never been much interested in the Lakes but she was quite good at map reading and geography and somehow she persuaded the party to abandon their planned journey and to visit Pemberley instead. The jaunt was arranged with perfect timing, their arrival coinciding with Darcy's return from visiting the Bingleys in London. And after just one glimpse of Pemberley, Elizabeth forgot revenge and was very much in love. Her flashing eyes and sparkling wit ensured that Darcy was her slave and not long after both he and Bingley were back at Netherfield and queuing up to bargain with my father. Integral to the bargaining was the fate of lanky Lydia. Alas, poor Lydia.

Shortly after the militia left Meryton, Lydia, initially in love with the entire regiment, had, in competition with our sister Kitty, at least one eye reserved for Mr Wickham. And, in pursuit of him (not unlike a rabbit setting out to catch a fox) and much to the chagrin of our sister Kitty, she inveigled an invitation to visit Brighton as the guest of Colonel and Mrs Foster. And finding Brighton a little dull and the sea air not really to her liking, she had most willingly accepted Reynard's proposal that they should set off together on life's long journey tying the knot eternal when and if they made it as far as Gretna. But the promptings of the blood proved to be too strong and their romantic journey ended in a two week love-in in a bawdy house in one of London's less salubrious suburbs. But all was to turn out well for Lydia too.

As by now I am sure all my readers know, Lydia ceased to be a fallen woman and Wickham a renowned rake following the intervention of our white knight Mr Darcy. Darcy and Wickham, who had grown up as virtual brothers, were now to be eternal brothers-in-law. And on ten thousand pounds a year, Fitzwilliam Darcy could afford to settle his brother's debts and secure a marriage settlement.

Lydia was in her seventh heaven and on visiting Longbourn was heard to boast, 'Who would have thought that I, the youngest, would be the first to marry and even earlier, the first to lose her maidenhead?' The shameless little hussy.

But Lydia was not the first to lose her virginity.

No. I had lost mine some six months earlier. It happened at

a servant's masked ball held in the town hall at Meryton. I had gatecrashed in the guise of Quasimodo and had caught the eye of an old flame. It was Grandison our sometime gardener. And while the Roger de Coverley was in full swing, he had taken me and my maidenhead together in the cellarage beneath the hall. With no foreplay, no after-play, and very little in between, it was not a particularly pleasurable experience. Certainly much less enjoyable than self-pleasuring or, dare I say it, masturbation.

Through masturbation I had found my inner self and, soon after, I decided that I would become a writer, and would be wedded eternally to my books.

Ah masturbation, that balancing of yin and yang, that wonderful moist conductivity to the centre.

4

Elizabeth: Sex Comes to Pemberley

The Darcys had lived for generations on the Pemberley estates, there in the woods and meadows where the Erewash twists sluggishly through alder trees, separating Derbyshire from Nottinghamshire. It was said that the first of the family, Philip d'Arcy, had come over to England with William the Conqueror and had been awarded land for his services. The Darcys were a taciturn, dark-haired people, slow to take offence but even slower to forgive once offence had been taken. Until the middle of the eighteenth century, they had been simple landed gentry, living comfortably but unostentatiously off the income accruing from their land. Elder sons had inherited and had become landlords. Younger sons had often led more distinguished lives: some in battle; some as ministers at court; others as practitioners of the law.

When it was rumoured that a canal might be built between Chesterfield and Derby, Fitzwilliam Darcy's grandfather had sold a substantial portion of his property and had invested in a large plantation in Antigua. From this moment the family's financial security was assured. His son had made considerable improvements to the house and the surrounding park and with the income accruing from their sugar plantation there had been no need for his heirs to engage in any form of occupation.

Before leaving Longbourn, Elizabeth had gleaned a little of this history and as their carriage wound its way down the country lanes, she watched for the first appearance of Pemberley with some perturbation; and when at length they turned in at the lodge, her spirits were in a flutter. The park was very large. They entered it at one of its lowest points, and drove for some time through a beautiful wood stretching beside undulating meadowland. Heaven and earth were teeming around them and Elizabeth could feel the sap in the spring air. It had rained heavily the night before and it almost seemed as though the fresh bright sunshine was being drawn into the breast and bowels of the surrounding landscape.

Her mind was too full for conversation, but she saw and admired every remarkable spot and point of view. While her aunt and her uncle were expressing both their wonder and their admiration, Elizabeth had time to reflect. Her brief relationship with Darcy passed through her mind in much the same way as it is said that an entire life can pass before the eyes of a man while he is drowning.

There was that first fatal meeting at the ball in Meryton, where she had heard him reject his friend Bingley's suggestion that he should dance with her. 'Tolerable, but not handsome enough to tempt *me*,' had been Darcy's judgement. Just 'tolerable?' In Meryton? And she remembered the following days and nights at Netherfield Park, when she had tended Jane in her illness, aware that Bingley's sisters were maliciously sneering at her, but that Darcy's eyes were on her constantly. 'Why?' she had wondered. 'Why me?' Then there was Wickham's story, telling her all that she wanted to hear about this haughty, aloof, insulting man and serving to confirm all her prejudices about him. And then there were their meetings at Hunsford and at Rosings, culminating in his quite extraordinary proposal, a companion piece to that of her cousin, Mr Collins. 'In vain I have struggled. It will not do. My feelings will not be repressed. You must allow me to tell you how ardently I admire and love you.' Admiration and love to be followed by an apology for both his passion and his proposal, his sense of her inferiority and his awareness of the degradation that the connection must bring to him and to the name of Darcy.

The carriage gradually ascended for half-a-mile, and they found themselves at the top of a considerable eminence, where the wood ceased, and the eye was instantly caught by Pemberley House, situated on the opposite side of a large lake. It was a handsome stone building, standing well on rising ground, and backed by a ridge of woody hills. Elizabeth was delighted. She had never seen a place where art and nature had come together more graciously. Her aunt and her uncle were warm in their admiration; and at that moment she felt that to be mistress of Pemberley might indeed be something! And to think that she had momentarily toyed with the notion of marrying the philanderer Wickham. How easily she had been deceived and how reprehensible now her hotheadedness seemed.

They descended the hill, crossed the bridge, and drove to the door. On applying to see the place, they were admitted into the hall by the housekeeper, a respectable-looking elderly woman, who introduced herself as Mrs Reynolds. The hall was a large, well-proportioned room, handsomely fitted. Elizabeth, after slightly surveying it, went to a window to enjoy its prospect. Every disposition of the landscape was good; and she looked on the whole scene – the river, the lake, the trees scattered on its banks – with delight. The rooms which followed were lofty and gracious and their furniture suitable to the fortune of its proprietor. She noted, with interest, a set of uniquely designed colonial chairs, featuring traditional motifs, such as pineapples, fish and stylised serpents. This, she thought, was a potentially embarrassing trace of the West Indian connection. But taken as a whole, the Darcy taste was impeccable. It was neither gaudy nor uselessly fine and showed less splendour but more real elegance, than the furniture of Rosings.

'And of this place,' she thought, 'I might have been mistress. With these rooms I might now have been familiarly acquainted and, instead of viewing them as a stranger, I might have rejoiced in them as my own and welcomed to them as visitors my uncle and aunt. But no,' recollecting herself, 'had I accepted Darcy, by his terms, my uncle and aunt would have been lost to me; I should never have been permitted to invite them here.'

'I have heard much of your master's fine person,' said Mr Gardiner, whose easy and pleasant manners encouraged communicativeness, and Mrs Reynolds, either by pride or attachment, had evidently great pleasure in talking of her master. 'Oh, he is the best of men and the best of brothers,' she replied. 'I have never known a cross word from him in my life, and I have known him ever since he was four years old.' 'Is your master much at Pemberley in the course of the year?' asked Mrs Gardiner. 'Not so much as I could wish, but I dare say he may spend more of his time here now that Miss Darcy is always down for the summer months.' 'Except,' thought Elizabeth, 'when she goes to Ramsgate.' 'If your master were to marry, might you then see more of him?' asked Mr Gardiner. 'Yes, sir; but I do not know when *that* will be. I do not know of a lady who is good enough for him.' Elizabeth almost stared at her. 'Can this be my Mr. Darcy?' she wondered.

In the picture-gallery of the great house there were many family portraits. Here, present, past and future met in an instant. The portraits of Darcy's forebears seemed to sneer down at Elizabeth, suggesting that she, devoid of heritage, was nothing. There were Judges, Admirals, Generals, all dignified in their regalia. They gazed down on her, their eyes saying: 'No breeding'; 'common'; 'commoner than a commoner'; 'quite unworthy of the house of Darcy'; 'you, Elizabeth Bennet, are nothing'. Initially she was cowed, but then her soul rebelled. 'You may have had your moments of pomp and pride,' she thought, 'but now it is you who are faded into nothingness and all that remains of you is an attitude, a smear of the past. Whereas I, I have life.'

Then she was arrested by a more modern portrait, which had a striking resemblance to Mr Darcy himself. It seemed to smile down on her as she remembered Darcy smiling when they had last met. And as she met the portrait's gaze, she became half aware of a strange tingling in her loins. She stood for several minutes before the picture, imagining what might have been and sensing darkly the doom, the doom and the emptiness to come.

She saw her future ahead of her, she, as a lonely spinster, a lonely, though doubtless popular aunt, devoting much of her time to her sister's children. And she might, had she been less wilful, have been viewing Pemberley as the future Mrs Darcy. As a landlord and master, her master, how many people's happiness were in his guardianship! How much of pleasure or pain would it have been in his power to bestow! How much good or evil might be done by them together?

On leaving the house, Mr Gardiner, ever interested in fishing, expressed a wish to walk around the lake, a request which was most graciously granted.

As they headed towards the lakeside path, Elizabeth turned back to look at Pemberley once more; her uncle and aunt stopped also, and while the former was conjecturing as to the date of the building, who should suddenly come forward from the road, which led behind it to the stables? None other than Mr Darcy himself. They were within twenty yards of each other, and so abrupt was his appearance, that it was impossible to avoid his sight. Their eyes instantly met, and the cheeks of both were overspread with the deepest blush. He absolutely started, and for a moment seemed immovable from surprise; but recovering himself, he advanced towards the party, and spoke to Elizabeth, if not in terms of perfect composure, at least of perfect civility. The Gardiners exchanged glances and, after embarrassed introductions, moved on ahead to provide the young couple with some semblance of privacy.

They walked on together in silence, each of them deep in thought. Elizabeth was not comfortable; that was impossible; but she was flattered and pleased; and she was aware that now not only her face was flushed. They entered the woods, the welcoming woods, and bidding adieu to the lake for a while, ascended to higher ground. The opening of the trees gave the eye power to wander, over many charming views of the lake and the opposite hills, with the long range of woods overspreading the whole landscape. They paused for a moment, gazing at the scene before them, aware that they were now quite alone. They could just hear the far away receding chatter of Mr and Mrs Gardiner, and the nearer, seemingly eternal lapping of the water at the lake's edge. Darcy turned to her and gazed into her eyes, the gaze of a man determined to know his destiny. And Elizabeth met his gaze with just a hint of laughter in her eyes. A witticism flickered through her mind, but deep down she knew that this was not a time for banter. Words would be meaningless and stale. She lowered her face as if to consent to the importunity of his will.

He did not speak, but took her gently by the hand and led her deeper into the wood, into a dark hollow where, like a shadow, the day had gone into a faintly luminous retreat. Elizabeth was just aware that pale drops of flowers glimmered under the hazel trees and she sensed that for a moment, if only for a moment, here was to be her Garden of Eden. She lifted her face to him, and he bent forward and kissed her on the mouth, gently, with a kiss that both knew to be an eternal pledge. And as he kissed her, his heart strained in his breast. He had never intended to love her. But now, at last, it was over. He had crossed over the gulf to her, and all that he had left behind had shrivelled and become void.

Then he took her in his arms and drew her to him, and suddenly she became small in his embrace, small and nestling, like a dove. All resistance to him was gone, quite gone, and she began to melt into him, melting into peace, a marvellous peace. Then softly, with a gentle swoon-like caress of his hand in pure soft desire, softly he stroked the silky slope of her silk clad loins, down, down, then rising, up towards her soft warm buttocks, coming nearer and nearer to the very quick of her. And she felt him like a flame of desire, cruel yet tender, and she felt herself melting in the flame as his manhood rose against her with such strange force and assertion. 'Oh, Mr Darcy,' she found herself saying in an involuntary sigh. But the 'Oh' was in no way a rebuke, more of an invitation. Then, lying back against the dark green sward, she yielded to him with a quiver that was like death. Gone was the old stable ego of the character; the Elizabeth Bennet of Longbourn, pert, pretty and witty, was no more. 'Lift me, lay me, now, now, now,' she heard herself cry. Then as he entered her with a strange slow thrust, not of triumph but of peace, she sensed his masculine power, ah, such power, the power which she thought must have made the world in the very beginning.

And now it seemed that she was like the lake in a high wind, nothing but dark waves rising and heaving, heaving with a great swell, so that slowly her whole self, her whole inner darkness, was in motion, rolling towards him in its dark, dumb mass. And he was a great bird, caught on the billows of the wind and the waves, and together they exulted in the hurl and the gliding as she abandoned the old self, the self so entwined in the drab quotidian world of Meryton and Longbourn. And he, heaving above her like some great storm fowl on palmy snow-pinions, was fire, pure, proud fire and she submitted to him her proud new Ledaean self. Oh, and then, far down inside the new self, the depths of her very being parted and rolled asunder, in long, deep, contented moans spreading out from the centre of her as the soft, soft plunging of the strange miraculous phallus went deeper and deeper, till suddenly, in a soft, shuddering convulsion, the quick of her was touched, and the Elizabeth Bennet of old petty rivalries and prejudices and minor meaningless triumphs, was undone. 'Ah so lovely, too lovely, too lovely,' she heard herself cry out in exaltation.

And now she was fully herself again and her body clung with tender love to him, and blindly to the wilting penis, as she felt it so tenderly, frailly, unknowingly withdraw from her, after the fierce thrusting of its potency. As it drew out and left her body, the secret, sensitive thing, she gave an unconscious cry of pure loss. It had been so perfect! And she loved him so! 'It was so lovely!' she moaned. 'It was so, so lovely!'

But he said nothing, only softly kissing her tenderly as he lay still above her. And she moaned with a sort of bliss, both as a sacrifice, and as a newborn thing. And now in her heart the strange wonder of him was awakened. No more Pride and no more Prejudice and no more hiding of their true feelings and desires.

And now she touched him. How beautiful he felt, how pure in tissue! How lovely, how lovely, strong, and yet pure and delicate, such stillness of the sensitive body! Her hands came timorously down his back, to the firm fine globes of his buttocks. Beauty! Such beauty! A sudden little flame of new awareness went through her. And she exulted in the life within life, the sheer warm, potent loveliness.

Then gradually the everyday world of time and hours and minutes and graded distinctions returned. Time to return, to return to the great house of Pemberley. They began their walk back in silence, each deep in thought. Darcy was first to break the silence. 'There is a person in my family who most particularly wishes to be known to you,' he said. 'Will you allow me, or do I ask too much, soon to introduce my sister to your acquaintance?' She turned to him and smiled, her smile signifying both gratitude and consent. 'And, oh yes,' he continued with some embarrassment, 'I will now have to introduce you more formally to my aunt, Lady Catherine.' 'It will be a pleasure to make the acquaintance of your sister,' said Elizabeth. 'But as for Lady Catherine de Bourgh, few families are without their embarrassing relatives.'

Elizabeth felt both pleased and flattered. Darcy's wish of introducing his sister to her was a compliment of the highest kind. And it was, she realised, a tacit proposal. On reaching the house they found Mr and Mrs Gardiner, waiting for them somewhat impatiently. Elizabeth exchanged knowing glances with her aunt. Darcy pressed them all to go into the house and partake of some refreshment. But the carriage was ready and they were already late, so the Gardiners declined.

As they drove off, the observations of her uncle and aunt now began; and each of them pronounced her Mr Darcy to be infinitely superior to anything they had expected. 'He is perfectly well behaved, polite, and unassuming,' said her uncle. 'There is something a little stately, perhaps rather stiff in him, to be sure,' replied her aunt, 'but it is confined to his air, and is not unbecoming. I can now say with the housekeeper, that though some people may call him proud, I have seen nothing of it. I was never more surprised than by his behaviour to us. It was more than civil; it was really attentive; and there was no necessity for such attention. His acquaintance with Elizabeth was anything but trifling.' Elizabeth, yet again, exchanged glances with her aunt. 'To be sure, Lizzy, he may not be quite as handsome as your Wickham; or, rather, he has not your Mr Wickham's countenance, though his features are perfectly good. But how came you to tell me that he was so haughty and disagreeable?' Elizabeth smiled knowingly.

As their carriage ascended the hill making its way towards the entry gate, Elizabeth looked back on Pemberley. The evening mists were rising now and in the broad expanse of tranquil light she saw a faint band of iridescence which seemed, even as she watched, to gather into itself mysteriously as it formed into a vast rainbow whose great arc framed both house and lake. And in the arch of the rainbow she saw a new beginning and knew there would be no shade or shadow of a further parting.

5

Jane's Journal

Volume 1

4th September. Dinner in Meryton. Roast leg of mutton, trout and an abundance of wine and then port. Mother quite tipsy and going on and on about the new tenant of Netherfield. Thirteen at the table. Unlucky. Uncle unwell. Yet another ague. They called in Slop who has moved into leeches and bled him copiously. £2 for the visit and a shilling for each of the leeches. Much talk of the militia – though no one invited. On returning home, another family row. Father says that Mother and Lydia drink too much wine. Mother swore by God and by all the angels that she never drinks more than five glasses a day and immediately fainted just to prove it. Lydia supporting mother and both in tears.

8th September. Another rainy day. How I love the rain. I love the feeling on my face. In the early morning walked to Lucas Lodge. C still in bed. Went upstairs and lay beside her. Then a tremendous thunder storm. Vivid lightning and tremendous peals of thunder. In the midst we drew closer together and made love and enjoyed one of the best kisses we have ever had. Then the heaviest rain that I can ever remember. The family row continues. Father has refused to call on Mr Bingley. Mother feigned yet another fainting fit.

15th September. C says our love must be kept secret. For how long? Perhaps forever. I asked her if she thinks that it is sinful. The Bible seems to say that love between two men is wicked. The Bible, C says, makes no mention of the love between two women. She says it is based on natural feeling and that natural feeling can't be wrong. The News from

London is that the King is mad again. Will the Prince of Wales now become Regent? C says there will be a new age of decadence. She tells me that her teeth are aching.

18th September. Flirted with a pretty girl as I walked in to Meryton. Her name is Anne Browne. C is now not the only one. I can do so much with just my eyes. Mary was with me and I suspect she may know. She says that I look like an innocent flower but really am a lurking serpent, like Elizabeth. She may be right. Perhaps I am in love with nobody but myself.

20th September. Did nothing but dream of Anne Browne. She is very pretty and seems to enjoy my attentions. I used to think my love for C would last forever. What beautiful blue eyes. I want her terribly. I feel unclean. But my desire is true. Should I be true to my desire? I owe much to my journal. It helps me to unburden my mind, like a good and patient friend.

24th September. C has had her tooth out. Had a very bad night in spite of 60 drops of laudanum. As I was about to leave she suggested a quick kiss. She bolted the door and I took off my pelisse and drawers, and got into bed with her and had a good kiss in less than seven minutes. Disturbed when Lady L knocked to ask how she had slept. But now, though I have spent the morning in her arms, I know that I really do not love her. Yet I know that I cannot lie alone in my own bed and not imagine her there beside me.

25th September. Supper at Meryton. Sweetbreads, pheasant, scalloped oysters, mashed potatoes, hot apple tarts and stewed pears. Afterwards toasted cheese. Uncle much improved and again drinking too much wine.

28th September. Feeling very guilty. Made Charlotte a nosegay of flowers. Tried to kiss, but C dry as a stick.

1st October. More about our 'Prince Charming'. Father has visited Mr Bingley and says he seems amiable. Just right for

Elizabeth, I thought. But mother has other ideas. He has promised that he will return the visit and that he will attend the coming ball in Meryton. Uncle Phillips, dangerously ill again. Dr Slop had him bled in the temple with a lancet and then ten more leeches. He now sleeps all day.

2nd October. I slept badly again last night. I feel trapped, at times almost suffocated. Mr Bingley rode over to repay father's visit. Not allowed to meet him but we all peered down at him through an upstairs window. Lydia giggling, Kitty coughing. Poor Kitty. How tired I am of listening to that cough. It seems to vibrate up and down my spine. And at times Lydia's giggling is even worse. Mr Bingley made a smart arrival, black horse and blue coat, but rather short. Or so Lizzy says. After ten minutes with father in the library he left. Mother in raptures and now ready to die happy. No wonder I feel suffocated.

3rd October. I woke early. A long talk to C. Says she knew she was different at fifteen at Miss Knight's school. Walking home I smiled again at Miss Browne. I think she may have been waiting for me.

8th October. Another early visit to C and this time two long, long kisses. C's room is like an eyrie, as though in another world. A little heaven. C says that Lady L is behaving just like mother and can only talk of Netherfield Park and Mr Bingley. She thinks that C must be in the reckoning, as the Lucas title is even better value than the Bennet looks. Mr Bingley is bringing down a large party to the ball to help protect him from the merry girls of Meryton. Or perhaps to provide us all with husbands.

October 10th. At breakfast father posed the problem. Why has an eligible young man from London rented an estate in Hertfordshire? Mother thinks he is looking for a wife. Mother thinks all rich young men are looking for wives. But why in Meryton? Surely there are enough pretty young fortune hunters in London?

October 12th. Dreamed that I was lying with C and that she showed me that she had a penis. Very small. Not unlike a leach.

October 19th. How I hate balls. And men. How I wish that I could leave off being young and pretty and marriageable and were an elderly ugly spinster who could sit by the fire and drink as much wine as I liked. Like Miss Davis.

Mr Bingley there with his two sisters, one a Mrs Hurst. Both elegant and beautiful. Too many women as usual. Some stood up with each other. Very common. Mr B began by asking Charlotte and I saw Lady Lucas smiling as though they already were engaged. I stood up with him twice. Had little to say, so we just smiled and smiled. B's friend Mr Darcy wears a perpetual sneer. 'Just right for Elizabeth,' I thought 'till he insulted her, whispering in a loud voice that she was 'barely tolerable.' The older sister, Mrs Hurst, kept giving me the look. I smiled back. Her husband dresses like a bishop but looks and acts just like a pig, no time for dancing, just for gobbling and gulping. I do feel better for this writing. Throwing my mind on paper always seems to do me good.

October 20th. A cold, ugly day but Mother in her element. Described last night's ball in great detail to poor father who winced and retired to the library. Lydia and Kitty think Bingley rather too short, especially for Lydia. We all hate Mr Darcy. Family harmony at last.

October 21st. A visit from the Lucas family. Much talk about Mr Bingley and Mr Darcy. Mother commended C for being B's first choice. Lady L repaid the compliment by saying that she had heard that Mr B said that I was the prettiest at the ball. Commiserations with Lizzy. 'Only barely tolerable'. C said that Darcy has a reason to be proud. 'He has everything in his favour.' Young George Lucas a great supporter. 'If I were as rich as he is I would keep a pack of fox hounds and drink a bottle of wine every day.' Mother rather shocked and very righteous. You would think she had never touched a glass.

October 25th. The rain has let up at last. Mr Bingley's sisters called on us. Both very attentive to me – but I think for different reasons. In the evening I went out alone into the garden. The sky was starry and it was very cold. The trees and the grass looked very strange, quite unreal. I could not help thinking of Louisa Hurst.

October 27th. Another early visit to the Lodge. Charlotte determined that I should do what I can to entrap poor Mr Bingley. She says, 'your Bingley.' Marriage, she says, is the lesser of two evils, worse to be an eternal spinster. 'Happiness in marriage is entirely a matter of chance,' she says. 'Well, you marry Mr Bingley,' I answered. I said I could not like men and that I will never marry. After a long talk we tried to kiss, but C again rather too dry. On my walk back home smiled again at Miss Browne. If only one could tell false love from true love as one can tell toadstools from mushrooms.

November 1st. England is now at war with Sweden. And Mrs K's son reported dead in France. Lydia glad we have the militia. Mary says we have no need as we are an island fortress. Why are we at war with three countries and on three different fronts? Men. Men. Men or as a Latin poet might say, Male. Male. Male.

November 3rd. Dinner and dancing at Lucas Lodge. B again all smiles and very attentive to everyone. Mr Darcy seemed to take notice of Elizabeth who refused to dance but then flirted with him all evening. Mary took over at the piano and bored us with her new concerto. Very long. Plays mechanically well but with no real feeling. There are times when I loathe my whole family – even Elizabeth.

November 12th. More rain. Invited to dinner at Netherfield. Mother made me ride there alone. Dinner followed by cards and rather formal. Mr Hurst dresses like a dandy and lives only for his cards and for his food. Poor Louisa. I kept smiling at her. Weather too foul to return so I spent the night. After retiring, a tap on the door, and there – not unexpected – was Louisa. We lay together and talked for over an hour. Never should have married Hurst. She would not elaborate. Yet again family pressure? Woke with all the signs of a bad cold coming.

November 15th. I dreamed that Charlotte came to me in my bed. I kissed her but her flesh felt cold. And then when I looked down on her she was severely pale and then I realised that she was dead.

Sunday 17th. Back at Longbourn at last. Lizzy has been sweet and attentive to me all week and rather flirtatious to Mr Darcy. He looks like a bewildered animal. Mother in seventh heaven. I am missing Louisa. She is so beautiful that I now cannot see any other beauty. When she speaks to me and laughs I feel I understand God.

Monday 18th. Today we met our cousin, the Reverend Collins. Very plain and very pompous. He looks on Longbourn and all our family as his own private possessions. Mother now has him earmarked for Elizabeth. Mother had a long chat to me about Mr Bingley. She says he could be the ending of the anxiety of the entail, providing her with the security she will need when father dies. Not in those exact words. Did I, could I, love him? I just smiled. But, No. No. NO.

Tuesday 19th. On our walk back from Meryton, we met a Captain Wickham. Lydia and Kitty had met him on an earlier visit and had spoken excitedly about him. Very charming and flirted with Elizabeth. He didn't seem to notice me. Why did I feel jealous? I know that I cannot live happily without female company, without someone to interest me. But still I felt just a little jealous.

Wednesday 20th. Supper with Aunt Phillips. Uncle again in bed. Much talk of Mr Wickham. He has now taken over from Captain Carter as the family's favourite. Lydia, Kitty, and, I suspect, Elizabeth are all in love with him. Not a good match as he has no family and no real prospects. Just charm and good looks. I am starting to think like Charlotte.

Thursday21st. An early morning visit from Caroline and Louisa. Both looking very elegant. But for their different styles of dressing they could well be twins. Though Louisa's face is more spiritual, less worldly. Mother very vulgar. Talking quite openly about me and Mr Bingley. I feel low and mortified and unhappy and wretchedly ashamed. How I loathe my family.

Friday 22nd. It is late night. Very dark. Not a star to be seen. Early this morning I visited Charlotte. Not much conversation before getting into bed. It has been nearly three weeks. I spoke about Mr Bingley and lamented what now starts to seem to be my fate. I told her that I would never marry and that I cannot and will never like men. Was I being too strident? There is something to be said for a comfortable life away from mother. Until father dies, of course.

Saturday 23rd. Did nothing but dream of Miss Browne. Why Miss Browne? I thought that I loved Louisa. But Miss Browne is very pretty. And very young. Less worldly than Charlotte or Louisa. I realise now that Charlotte, though she can put on a sweet expression, is not pretty, really rather plain, but she has wonderful hands. She spent an age listening to our cousin Mr Collins and encouraging him in his pomposity.

Tuesday 26th. Another dreary but very showy ball, this time at Netherfield and hosted by Mr Bingley. At least twenty different sorts of wine and all sorts of fruit, some from France and some from Portugal. Mr Bingley's sisters call him Charles. Mr Collins threw himself at Elizabeth, insisting on the first two dances. Dancing is not one of his accomplishments. He spent the whole time stumbling and apologising. Mr Wickham not present in spite of his assurances. After her bouts with cousin Collins, Lizzie seemed relieved to be asked to dance by Mr Darcy. Again, Mr Bingley stood up with me twice. We smiled at each other and discussed the weather. I fear he may be starting to think that he's in love. But the family did what they could to allay his passion. Katie and Lydia whirled the militia off their feet. Mr Collins accosted Mr Darcy and preached to him about his Lady Catherine. Mary tried to sing. And mother's whispers to Lady Lucas about Bingley and me must have been heard by the whole assembly. I sense that I am about to lose all contact with Louisa.

Wed 27th. This morning an early visit from Mr Collins who asked to be alone with Elizabeth. Katie and Lydia, both giggling, tried to eavesdrop but were swept away by mother. When Eliza reported back that she had turned him down, there was a full family row. Mother took the refusal as a personal affront and fainted several times. Then Catherine and Lydia both turned him down without having been invited. 'He's so, so, ugly,' said Lydia. Thank goodness for my Mr Bingley. Mother has now decided that our Mr Collins might be just right for Mary. A walking, talking, Fordyce almanac.

Thurs 28th. A note from Louisa saying that the full party were about to leave unexpectedly for London and that she hoped that she and I might meet there. Very strange, but not really unexpected. No explanations given. Mother in a state of high consternation. Father assumes my heart must be broken – a situation calling for yet more wit. I smiled at him a little sadly. I won't miss their Mr Bingley, but I will miss not seeing my Louisa. At dinner, after at least five glasses of red wine, mother began to indulge in a lament about the entail. 'What will I do, Mr Bennet, when you die and I have little income, and no home and five great daughters to support?' Father pretended to console her by suggesting that if she continues drinking she might well die before him. As usual he was witty. 'Do not give way, my dear, to such gloomy thoughts, all may be well, my dear, and I might yet outlive you.'

Sat 30th. I visited Charlotte on my early morning walk. She seemed to be in mourning. We kissed uncomfortably. Then the truth. Yesterday our Mr Collins called on her and with Lizzy's rejection still ringing in his ears, he proposed and she accepted. She said again that she has come to regard marriage as the lesser of two evils. She says that our love can continue. I think she may have been planning this for days, if not weeks. Marriage? Possibly. With Mr Collins, no, no, no, never. Charlotte says she is suffering much from piles and that for some time she has feared that I no longer love her. I kissed her breasts and then realised that neither she nor her room seemed very sweet to me – or to my nose.

Back at Longbourn, I realised that Charlotte is and always has been worldly. And she has used me. How could I have adored her? She is not the angelic being I first thought or imagined. And I suspect now that she has secretly always preferred Elizabeth, at least as a companion. And she really is rather plain. I feel dirty and rejected. But I will not become guilty of adultery. Not with Charlotte.

But am I not as bad or even worse, allowing my fancies to dwell on other younger and much prettier women?

Monday, 2nd December. Visited Charlotte and I said it must end. She wept. But I will never, never, never visit her in Hunsford.

Wednesday 4th. Dreamed again about Anne Browne, meeting her on a walk, taking her into a shed and being connected to her. Imagined myself in men's clothing and having a very long thin penis. All this is very bad. My mind's not right. Must turn over a new leaf.

Thursday 5th. Walked into Meryton, hoping I might see Miss Browne. She was there as I had hoped. I stopped to talk to her. She has a common voice and rather vulgar manners. And she is engaged to be married in the spring to a farmer from Oakham.

Saturday 7th. Dreamed of Charlotte and our Mr Collins in connubial embrace. She is really very, very plain. An abundance of leeches in my dream. Leeches everywhere on them both. Perhaps they are well suited. How I need my journal. It has become my other self. When I speak to others, my thoughts are always edited and censored and framed by my artificial pretty smile.

Tuesday 10th. Found two hedgehogs in the garden. Took them a plate of gooseberries and a saucer of milk. Life must continue.

Monday 23rd. Aunt and Uncle Gardiner and their maid, Tyb, and their children have all arrived for Christmas. Aunt G is very wise. How unlike mother. The children docile and seem to like me. I showed them the hedgehogs. But I cannot see myself as a mother.

Tuesday 24th. Lizzy says that Aunt G has strongly advised her against any liaison with Mr Wickham. Lizzy senses that our aunt feels that he is shallow and a fortune hunter. Though who would look to the Bennet daughters for a fortune? Perhaps he has not yet heard about the entail. I am meant to be heartbroken which amuses me inwardly and father outwardly. He much prefers his jokes and witticisms to his wife or to any of his children.

Monday, 30th December. A huge relief. I am to accompany my aunt and uncle to London. The Bingley sisters made it clear that they thought that Cheapside, like its name, is somewhat unsalubrious. But my uncle has chosen to live where he still makes his money. It will be a relief to move away from a household in semi mourning – and mother is sure that I will somehow meet Mr Bingley and that all may yet be well. Surely no one ever doted on another as I did on Charlotte? I fondly thought our love and happiness would last forever. Alas, how changed. She is about to marry a dullard and a bore and just for the sake of security. But I am still miserable from trying to wean my heart from her. And I do believe that she still loves me. It will be a relief to go to London if only to miss the wedding. Writing my journal always does me good. I feel better now. I have gradually written myself from moody melancholy to contented cheerfulness.

Volume 2

Jan 1st. A new volume and I hope a new voice. I can and will tell my journal that which I can tell no one else. Without Charlotte, it is now my closest and perhaps my only, friend. Who am I? That question will be the subject of this, my second, journal. I am Jane Bennet, spinster. I think I will always be a spinster. I am twenty-two. From the moment of my birth, my mother and my father have looked on me as the answer to the entail. My face, a younger version of my mother's, or so they tell me, will be my fortune. Not my fortune. The family fortune. Mother's salvation. From the moment of my birth I have been moulded just for marriage. Cursed with a pretty face, as an infant I was taught to smile and smile and to lisp only 'please' and 'thank you', not even 'yes' and 'no'. It is as though I am a doll who has been designed by a committee, my mother and my father and my aunts. My face is pretty but my mirror tells me that my body is not beautiful. My breasts are somewhat undeveloped and are rather too small and my hips are wide and getting wider. Nothing which can't be controlled by the dress maker's art. I look around me and see other dolls. Elizabeth is not as pretty so has had to develop wit and archness and bright eyes in compensation. Kitty is pretty, but rather too pale. And is always coughing. Consumptive? Perhaps. And Lydia? She is young, has something of Elizabeth's vitality but is cruder and less witty. And Mary? Poor Mary has not a trace of what they call the Bennet looks. She really is very, very ugly.

My aunt and uncle seem to me to be an ideal married couple.My aunt is fine looking but is not vain and has chosen to cultivate her mind and not her face. And my uncle is sensible and intelligent, less witty but much more warm than my father. I think I will enjoy my time in London.

January 4th. Took a morning walk down and around Gracechurch Street. In Cannon Lane, I saw a pretty girl and desire rather overcame me. She returned my smile. I mentioned her to Tyb, my aunt's maid. Tyb says that she is probably 'a harlot'. Tyb is the daughter of a clergyman and is very poor. Poor girl, her face will never be her fortune and she will be doomed to work out her whole life in service. She will never be a harlot. Sat down to dinner at 7.30. Gravy soup, soles and beefsteaks, tart and cheese and a bottle of sherry. I drank a full two glasses and should sleep well. Good conversation, but the Phillips keep a better table.

January 5th. I sent a note to Louisa who lives in Grosvenor Street, inviting her to visit me. I suspect she will not answer. She and Caroline both seemed to sneer when I told them about my having relations who live in Cheapside. Not the place for London gentry – though their family's fortune was also made in trade. Less honest trade, I now suspect, than is my uncle's.

January 7th. This morning, not long after breakfast a carriage drew up outside our lodgings. It was Louisa. We walked and talked. She says she has become a 'club widow'. Mr Hurst now spends all his days and nights at Boodles, which is a London gambling club, so she is free to 'entertain' whoever and whenever she chooses. She says that the pretty girls who stand in Cannon Street are all prostitutes. They can, she thinks, earn as much as a sovereign a day. Some rent or even own their rooms. But proper gentlemen go to brothels, where they pay more but are less likely to contract diseases. Louisa is very worldly. I will try to arrange to visit her early next week.

January 9th. If I had not come to London, today I would have attended Charlotte's wedding. Guests for dinner, a Sir John Smith and his wife. I think my aunt wanted to show me that they move in good society. Sir John is a large, good humoured, over-talkative man. He tends to dominate the conversation, aping good humour if not good manners. He could just pass muster as a gentleman, though both his money and his title have been made in trade. Lady S is quiet and smiles a lot. I suspect that by being silent she escapes vulgarity. Sir John and I both acknowledged that we keep journals and we promised not to note down anything against each other. He taught me a simple code to ensure that my most intimate thoughts can be kept forever secret. Bir l fiis vwfubbubf. Could not sleep for several hours. Then I dreamed of Charlotte and of Anne Browne and when I woke I thought I was in the arms of my Louisa.

January 12th. I have been thinking much about the marriage market. Were I to stand in Cannon Street, I might earn my pound a day. But because my family is respectable, they say my face could be worth at least £20,000; Elizabeth, with her eyes and her vitality, may be worth £10,000 as Kitty may be and, if she is prudent, Lydia. Whereas poor Mary has been forced to develop righteousness in place of looks. Worthiness, even saintliness (which Mary has not) are not worth much. I remember Lizzy saying that what Mary needed was a clergyman – preferably a vkubs clergyman, she said in our father's voice.

January 19th. I told my aunt and uncle that I was going out to visit an old friend from Longbourn – and I took a cab and directed him to Grosvenor Street where Louisa was waiting for me. The house is showy, suggesting money, but not good taste. After taking coffee, Louisa took my hand and suggested that we retreat together to her upstairs apartment where we would be well away from all the servants. I smiled at her, my prettiest smile, but declined her invitation. Louisa is a married woman and though she does not love her husband, to make love to her would be sinful.

January 23rd. Spent the complete day with my Louisa. She collected me in her carriage and showed me what she called scenes of dissipation and vice. In Covent Garden there were rows and rows of young woman out to sell themselves, and in broad daylight. We drove across the Thames to a point where there were three gibbets, a corpse hanging from each. Louisa told me they had been Malay sailors sentenced to death for murdering their captain. Then we went on to Grosvenor Street where again I told her that I could never love a married woman. She was very persuasive – memories of Charlotte. Before leaving, Louisa showed me a bowl of hyacinths. 'How lovely,' I said. 'Now you have learned to love a hyacinth and have gained a new source of enjoyment,' she said, 'and in life it is as well to have as many holds upon happiness as possible.'

January 28th. Dreamed all night of lying with Louisa. When I awoke, I dressed and walked to Mary Le Bow, the great church in Cheapside. I knelt and prayed for guidance. My mind kept racing. It says in the Bible that adultery is a sin. But it also says that it is sinful just to desire the love of a married woman. So am I already a sinner? If so, why not sin in deed as well as in thought? Is it not more sinful to marry a man you do not love? Poor Louisa is already damned. Perhaps we are doomed to be damned forever. Qgt bir vw slnbws rifwrgwe?

January 29th. Last night a violent longing for a female companion came over me. Never remember feeling it so painfully before. Like a fever

February 1st. Another visit to Louisa. We were alone, again in the great house. She asked if we might lie down and talk together as we had talked when she first visited me that night in Netherfield. She told me that she felt the need for some kind of confession. How could I refuse her? We went upstairs to her apartment and lay in each other's arms and talked. I should say that she talked and that I just listened. She told me that her brother and her husband are not as they had seemed at Netherfield Park. Poor Charles, she said, had tried to please his family by liking girls. But ever since his days at Eton, he has been what she cruelly terms a 'sodomite'. At Eton he was something of an outsider, too sensitive for the harshness of a public school regime, but young and pretty and much desired by older boys. Sodomy was rife. For some it was just a stage in growing up. But not for Charles. And then just over a year ago, Charles had met Mr Hurst at a nearby Molly House. 'What,' I asked, 'is a Molly House?' Louisa looked at me as though I was unusually innocent – or perhaps just ignorant. A 'molly,' she told me, is an effeminate man who likes to dress in women's clothing. And a Molly House is an inn or a tavern where mollies meet and Charles had met Jeremy, her Mr Hurst, at such a place not far from Grosvenor Street. Charles is not a molly but not only had the two men fallen in love, but they had been secretly married. Yes, married. At the Molly House in Vere Street one of the regulars was an ordained member of the Church of England. He, the very Reverend John Church, claims to have been visited by an angel in a dream and told that he would be the first of many to marry man to man and woman to woman. And there had been several marriages at Vere Street – all the participants being sworn to secrecy. By this time I was reeling. I tried hard to believe her story and was almost ready to give way to her entreaties, but we lay together most chastely for well over an hour.

February 3rd. Further revelations. I had so many questions. 'Why had Louisa posed as Mrs Hurst?' I asked. It had been an agreed and convenient deception. Charles had long realised that Louisa liked girls not men. And the trio had arranged what was a second marriage. This guaranteed propriety and allowed the two men to live together. 'Why did Bingley choose to move from London to Netherfield?' I asked. This was a question often asked by my father. Louisa told me it was because of a now notorious London scandal. Shortly before

Bingley had rented Netherfield, the Molly House in Vere Street had been raided by Bow Street Runners and Charles and Jeremy were among several dozen 'visitors' who had been arrested. And there had been young boys there too. Charles and Jeremy had pleaded ignorance and, aided by a substantial bribe, they had been released. Soon after, to avoid the ensuing scandal, Charles had come down to Hertfordshire and had arranged to move to Netherfield. A wise move. Louisa then read me a long account of the Vere Street arrests and their aftermath. Some half a dozen of the group arrested, those too poor to bribe the Runners, had been pilloried in the Haymarket, where a large crowd, mainly women, had pelted them with rotten fish, dead cats and vegetables. Some 200 constables had been needed to restore order. Again we talked, but did not kiss.

Feb 6th. In the afternoon I had a long talk with my aunt about love and marriage. She says that there is no future or fulfilment for young women who do not marry and marry well. 'Use your beauty while it lasts'. Very worldly, like Charlotte. She is worried that Elizabeth might be overcome with passion and marry Wickham just for love.

Feb 7th. Spent the morning writing a long letter to Elizabeth, gently suggesting that I was 'brokenhearted' and hinting that I was missing Mr Bingley. If I were to marry Bingley, I had realised, my life could be spent living near Louisa.

Feb 12th. Spent the afternoon with Louisa. We retired to her apartment where at last we kissed. Wonderful Louisa. How could I feel shame? She is part woman, part cat, part sea creature. So lithe and so mysterious. So unlike Charlotte. A woman made for loving. After our first kiss we slept together in each other's arms. She woke with a start and said, 'Oh, don't leave me yet. Don't ever, ever leave me.' We kissed again. Then she spoke to me most eloquently: 'I have lived in hope, hope that you and I will grow old together and that as we age our love will grow stronger and stronger. I loved you the first moment that I saw you. Jane, my Jane, you cannot, you cannot, doubt the love of one who has waited for you so patiently. You, and you alone can give me all the happiness I care for and I pledge here and now that I will indeed be eternally constant to you, and will from this moment always regard you as my wife and you and you alone shall have every smile and every breath of tenderness I can offer. I am entirely and eternally yours.'

All is now clear in my mind. I will marry Mr Bingley and live with him and Louisa and I will never then be parted.

February 10th. Rislt Kiyua lbs O qwew nleeuws um l xwenibt ub felxwxgyexg arewwr. Qw qweq nleeuws vt rgw cwet ewcwewbs Higb Xgyexg.

Song for Louisa

Tiy glcw elcuagws nt gwler
Kiyual, nt swle ibw.
Tiy glcw elcuagws not gwler.
Qurg tiye wtwa lbs tiye kuoa.
Tiy lew ri nw l fleswb id aqwwr swkufgra.
Tiye tiybf vewlara lew kujw kukuwa,
Lbs tiye vewlrg ua aqwwrwe rglb qubw;
Tiye kuoa rlarw kujw rgw aqwwr hyuxw id rgw
    oinwfelblrw,
Lbs gibwt lbs nukj kyej ybswe tiye ribfyw.
Tiye ajub gla rgw agwwb lbs rgw aqwwr isiye id lookwa.
Tiye blcwk ua kujw l eiybs fivkwr, anwkkubf id nteeg.
Lbs tiye rgufga kwls ri rglr flrw.
Qguxg nt kuoa ybkixj.

Ahead there lies a new life – and no further need to keep a journal.

6

Cassandra Bennet: Ruminations

Yes because he never did a thing like that before as call me Cassie my dear Cassie ever since the marriage it has been Mrs Bennet this and Mrs Bennet that and always acting his lordship not allowing Lydia a single penny to buy a dress for her very own wedding and saying that there would be no visits to Longbourn when before our marriage he had kowtowed yes kowtowed to me and to my mother and his very own daughter poor sweet Lydia so young but so enchanting just as when he courted me and though with brighter prospects which had seemed brighter then but much less good looking than her Mr Wickham and had he been promised £2,000 a year he would have been as good a match as Bingley though with Netherfield and a house in London though spineless yes why did he kowtow yes kowtow to his friend that Darcy that Darcy as rich they say as Tarsus or Esaw no not yes Croesus though who knows who was Croesus and pretending to be high and mighty with his aunt Lady Catherine this and Lady Catherine that and had she not been pigheaded he would have been a catch for Lizzy but between them a double marriage and regular visits to Pemberley how many rooms and such views where he would have to be the host and not just so high and mighty the very idea that Jane and Elizabeth and Lydia and Kitty and even poor Mary somehow strange that the family looks always missed one there was Aunt Agatha always a spinster though bright and cheery but oh so pious I suppose because no man would look at her twice always going on about some dean or bishop and not good looking like all the others Jane even Mrs Long said was the prettiest what a fine woman Mrs Long with such polite nieces though not likely to be married with their fat bottoms and their snub noses and no fortunes such a plain family yes my face was my fortune not all faces think of Charlotte and the Lucas family he might be Sir William but her fat neck and long nose and always scheming and her father in trade who would have thought her best friend but all is well and even a title could not be worth the looks of Jane or even Elizabeth though her tongue too like her father might well have been a spinster like Aunt Agatha no family looks last longer than a title poor Mary all that time singing and even Lizzie plays better always serious but never smiling and yes it was her eyes that must have caught Mr Darcy funny that perhaps Sir Fitzwilliam Darcy or even Lord Darcy would never have been a friend of Mr Bingley plain Mr Bingley though good looking and those sisters always with their noses turned up and that Mr Hurst fish-faced and dressed like a Bishop and always eating or at the card table and their eyes on their brother protecting him from Jane how spineless to ignore his heart and even he yes when he was but twenty-three and courting me just like Lydia but not before the marriage no what about Hymen and waiting we always had to wait for Hymen was he also Greek sounds Greek like Croesus Hymen knits funny that wait for Hymen to knit and then he would unknit or break could it be the same I guess all men are the same waiting to unknit the yes yes that first night so clumsy and so shy but little pain though there was just a trace of blood I saw him look though nearly not a virgin after Tom sweet Tom and the next morning with that sick voice playing his highness always high and mighty and telling me that we were young and the next night again so cocky men learn so quickly and no more pain and perhaps it was then yes then that Jane sweet pretty Jane so like her mother but even more like Lydia and had Mr Wickham so charming and so gallant with always the right word to know just how a woman feels and before Mr

Bennet there had been Henry and Tom but unlucky to marry into one's own family but Tom had looks like Mr Wickham and what eyes and that moment in the carriage his hands under my petticoat but then came Mr Bennett always a good match but five daughters and no son and the entail who'd have thought and had he been a bit more careful and not always thinking of his books and when the fun was over yes Jane had been the lucky one born in wedlock and in love and soon it had been a duty always a duty but first Jane and then Elizabeth and then Mary poor Mary might have been a boy so serious because she knows no man would look at her not even her father her own father and as for Kitty too pale but now that Elizabeth is Mrs Darcy and who knows Lady Darcy when Lady Catherine ugly name de Bourgh well Mrs Bennet is better than Mrs Breen her face so vulgar and broad-featured or Mrs Briggs with her large eyes and long nose and such bad breath or those awful names with bottom in them Mrs Ramsbottom or Miss Ann de Bourgh with a white head of cabbage skinny thing with a turn in her eye or some other kind and there might be but that Miss Darcy little Miss Darcy also pale and thin but taller and with they say at least £30,000 without a fortune because no man would even see her let alone look at her twice without a fortune besides there's no danger with a priest though it was said that Wickham and was it Miss King with freckles and £10,000 yes or was it £20,00 but Lydia with just £1,000 I wonder those nights alone in London might she have love is strong and when you feel that way so nice all over you can't help yourself though that name Wickham might be a warning funny names Mr Bingley Mr Wickham Lady Catherine de Bourgh perhaps a warning wicked Wickham such good looks and such good breeding perhaps a changeling yes really a Darcy would he with Lydia alone in London not the end of the world not earthquakes let's have a bit of fun first not through want of trying with Tom

poor Tom so long ago must be old now and edging to get up
under my petticoats especially then still I like that in him
sweet Cassie my Cassie my dear Cassie perhaps Cassandra
not like Croesus though also Greek they say could see into the
future and there they were Jane and Elizabeth and Lydia all
married and he would not believe me lucky my good looks
and not his fortune too little set aside for one let alone five
daughters and no son so that Mr Collins with his Lady
Catherine this and Lady Catherine that and why not Mary
because of the entailment so perhaps Kitty and even Mary
takes all sorts I wonder perhaps a clergyman in London or
Pemberley perhaps there for a full twenty nights but no much
too young and fun loving whereas Mary might well be a nun
or yes a clergyman like Mr Collins and I remember in the
carriage I wore that new dress silk or was it muslin and I knew
and he had barely and did they stay together in the inn where
he had found them suppose their rooms were beside each
other and any fooling went on in one how lucky to have such
a brother still a Gardiner like Eve funny how names change
but never faces though he must be quite old now at first we
spent long hours in bed no fool like an old fool and all those
painted women I had my suspicions after Lydia now he never
wants to visit London though still very fond of oysters not too
old he said my Cassie my sweetest Cassie did it mean no not
too old to perhaps another perhaps an heir perhaps that's why
five daughters keep on trying and no longer any pleasure
perhaps if Hill will cook him oysters and when he comes in I'll
let down my hair he says I am still beautiful unlike Lady
Lucas or that nice Mrs Long or sister Phillips if men only knew
that even if looks don't last they last forever think of Lydia
who would have thought the first to marry and the youngest
but tall enough to be the first with lucky Wickham oh how
sweet lucky Wickham could he have done without for twenty
days in London unlike Tom I remember how he squeezed me

and I just pressed the back of his like that with my thumb to squeeze back then because he was so very handsome almost too beautiful for a man and then that girl was it Hessie we were like cousins what age was I then the night of the storm I slept in her bed she had her arms round me what fun and she kissed me six or seven times didn't I cry yes but Tom or was it Henry how I thought then we might become engaged and I was in fits of laughing with the giggles what would it be like with a Bishop or Mr Collins plain Mr like Fitzwilliam Darcy or with a coalman or a gardener Grandison strange name too grand for a gardener with those eyes always slyly glancing and then so suddenly with Miss Dickens who would have thought that all men are the same at first the pain and then yes yes quite wonderful and then it's just too ordinary same again but wicked Wickham would ruin any woman but not my Lydia my clever Lydia why can't you even kiss a man without first marrying him and that first kiss long and hot and down into the soul how I wish that some other man would take me sometime when he's not there and kiss me in his arms like Tom sweet Cassie kiss me wildly it's still there and there's nothing like a kiss long and hot and his hands are wrinkled now and when Tom I thought and yes he gave me that flower all women no all girls are flowers and Tom or was it Henry had picked the flower which was a lily and yes I thought his lips had a salty taste I wonder if he remembers now yes I remember that second night firm and strong my eyes half shut it's all books now and wise words but then three times and more quite like a stallion or a ram the animal in him but then come children and the dance is over old now but not the dreams yes the dreams yes the dreams still come when we are old now even Tom how he loved my hair and could he see me now I wonder if my sister Gardiner and the Gardiner name the Eve and Adam and I saw his eyes gazing at my feet and then I knew and when he said sweet Cassie

was he my sweet Cassie was he thinking that Jane and
Elizabeth my little Lizzie and Lydia and Catherine little Kate
might soon and even Mary who knows in London there might
be but not in Longbourn or in Pemberley was he thinking or
did he remember and I remember Tom's first kiss so salty so
like butter and his hand so near my drawers and I not then
sixteen like Eve and I bet he never saw a better pair of thighs
so white they are the smoothest place is right here between
this bit and here how soft like a peach easy God I wouldn't
mind being a man and get up on a lovely woman oh Lord
what a row who knows is there anything the matter with my
insides perhaps those sweetbreads Slop says less wine but old
now of course but that second night he came to me shaking
like a jelly and he wanted everything so quickly at first which
takes away the pleasure and afterwards he gave me flowers
yes eight large poppies but they died and when he came to me
I was not ready no time for powder I wonder if they had two
rooms two separate rooms in that inn and the the third night
I saw that thing like a stallion after I took off all my things
with the blinds down after my hours dressing and perfuming
and that face lotion my skin like new and it was like iron or
some kind of a thick crowbar standing all the time he must
have eaten oysters I think a few dozen nice invention they
made for women for them to get all the pleasure I wonder
they're not afraid of getting a kick or a bang or something
there the woman is beauty of course that's admitted placed up
there like those statues in the museums one of them
pretending to hide it with her hand they are so beautiful of
course compared with what a man looks like with his two
bags full and his other thing hanging down out of him or
sticking up at you like a hat rack no wonder they hide it with
a cabbage leaf but if someone gave them a touch of it
themselves they'd know what I went through with Jane and
that fourth night he didn't come though I had on my new

clean smock and then how short is pleasure yes we are like flowers but I can't help it if I'm young still it's a wonder I'm not an old shrivelled hag before my time living with him so cold never embracing me when Kitty marries what shall I wear shall I wear a white rose I love flowers I'd love to have the whole place swimming in roses God of heaven there's nothing like nature the wild mountains then the sea and the waves and rivers and lakes and flowers all sorts of shapes and smells and colours springing up even out of the ditches primroses and violets nature and he called me Cassie my sweet Cassie come again Cassie still old but not too old perhaps at Pemberley yes yes at Pemberley and I'll tell him with my eyes to ask again yes and then yes yes my mountain flower and first I'll put my arms around him yes and draw him down to me so he can feel my breasts all perfume yes and his heart will be going like mad and yes at Pemberley yes I will say again yes yes and he will say yes my sweet Cassie yes yes yes.

Coda: Saucy Sources – Suggestions for Further Reading

'Kitty in Love' is based on both the style and content of the 'Nausicaa' episode in James Joyce's *Ulysses*. On discovering that the fireworks display at the conclusion of the episode was a symbolic representation of an orgasm, an alert reader informed the 'New York Suppression of Vice' who presented a case against *Ulysses* in 1921. The book was declared obscene and banned. Throughout the 1920s, the United States Postal Services burned copies of the novel which was also banned in the United Kingdom until the early 1930s.

In 'Lusty Lydia' Kitty loses her Ulysses to her younger sister whose literary ancestor, Fanny Hill, post dates *Pride and Prejudice* by some thirty years. Though John Cleland's novel (one of the most prosecuted and banned books in history) has been celebrated and reviled as 'a synonym for obscenity' and as 'the first original English prose pornography', Fanny's situation as an innocent in London willingly seduced by a rake is not dissimilar to that of Lydia, alone with the wanton Wickham.

Mary's origins in 'Mary, Mary, Quite Contrary' and much of the prose style stem from *Tristram Shandy*. Sterne's novel gained its own kind of notoriety some years after its publication when a critic discovered that Sterne had incorporated into his text passages taken word for word from a range of works including Robert Burton's *The Anatomy of Melancholy*, Francis Bacon's *Of Death* and Rabelais's *Gargantua and Pantagruel*. Though some readers accused Sterne of plagiarism, others defended him for his innovations and he is now regarded as a father of inter-textuality. The Mary chapter of *Sex Comes to Pemberley* blends passages from *Tristram Shandy* with passages taken from Jane Austen's own *Juvenilia* in which the young Jane satirised the world and value systems of *Pride and Prejudice* with an anarchic teenage energy hardly hinted at in the final work. (Richard Jenkyns, a scholar and descendant of Jane Austen, compares his distinguished ancestor's *Juvenilia* with the writings of Laurence Sterne).

'Elizabeth: 'Sex Comes to Pemberley' begins and ends with passages based on the opening and closing paragraphs of *The Rainbow*. *The Rainbow*, now from time to time set as an A level text, was first published in 1915 and then, following an obscenity trial, was banned – all available copies being seized and burnt. The ban lasted for eleven years. However, the erotic climax of 'Love in a Landscape' is based on a much more notoriously banned book, *Lady Chatterley's Lover*. *Lady Chatterley's Lover* was first published in Italy in a private edition in 1928. Attempts to pave the way for unexpurgated editions resulted in obscenity trials and rejections in a number of countries including America, Australia, Canada, Japan and India. When, in 1960, Penguin risked prosecution by publishing the 'full, unexpurgated text' in England, this defiant gesture resulted in the now famous Lady Chatterley trial where, after receiving evidence from a range of literary and political figures, the book was declared to be of a literary merit which transcended any obscenity.

'Jane's Journal' is loosely based on the lesbian diaries of Anne Tyler. These diaries were written in the early years of the nineteenth century. Sexually explicit sections were written in an encrypted code. The diaries were hidden in Shibden Hall, the ancestral home of the Tylers, until they were found and deciphered at the end of the century by one of her descendants, John Lister. Lister ignored advice to burn the books but kept them concealed behind a panel in Shibden Hall. It was not until 1988 that the first selection from the diaries was made available to the general public. In June 2011, Anne Lister's diaries were recognized by the United Nations as a "pivotal" document in British history. (Helena Whitbread has transcribed Anne Lister's diaries and her edited selections are now available as: 'The Secret Diaries of Miss Anne Lister', now published by Virago, 2012; 'I Know My Own Heart', New York University Press, 1992; and 'No Priest But Love', Smith Settle, 1993.)

And back to *Ulysses*.

The book's final chapter, 'Cassandra Bennet: Ruminations,'centres on the memories and musings of a half asleep Mrs Bennet. The model for this chapter is the Penelope episode which concludes Joyce's novel.

Romance, erotica, sensual or downright ballsy. When you want to escape: whether seeking a passionate fulfilment, a moment behind the bike sheds, a laugh with a chick-lit or a how-to - come into the Bedroom and take your pick. Bedroom readers are open-minded explorers knowing exactly what they like in their quest for pleasure, delight, thrills or knowledge.